O'BRIEN panda cubs

PANDA CUBS SERIES
where reading begins

O'BRIEN SERIES FOR YOUNG READERS

 panda cubs

 pandas

 panda legends

 flyers

The Train Driver

Words: Kunak McGann
Pictures: Greg Massardier

THE O'BRIEN PRESS
DUBLIN

For Fiachra, my inspiration,
and for Joe, always

First published 2009 by The O'Brien Press Ltd,
12 Terenure Road East, Rathgar, Dublin 6, Ireland
Tel: +353 1 4923333; Fax: +353 1 4922777
E-mail: books@obrien.ie
Website: www.obrien.ie

ISBN 978-1-84717-083-5

British Library Cataloguing-in-Publication Data
A catalogue reference for this title is available
from the British Library

1 2 3 4 5 6 7 8 9 10
09 10 11 12 13 14 15

The O'Brien Press receives
assistance from

the arts
council
schomhairle
ealaíon

Typesetting, layout, editing: The O'Brien Press Ltd
Printing: KHL Printing Co Pte Ltd, Singapore

Can YOU spot the
panda cub
hidden in the story?

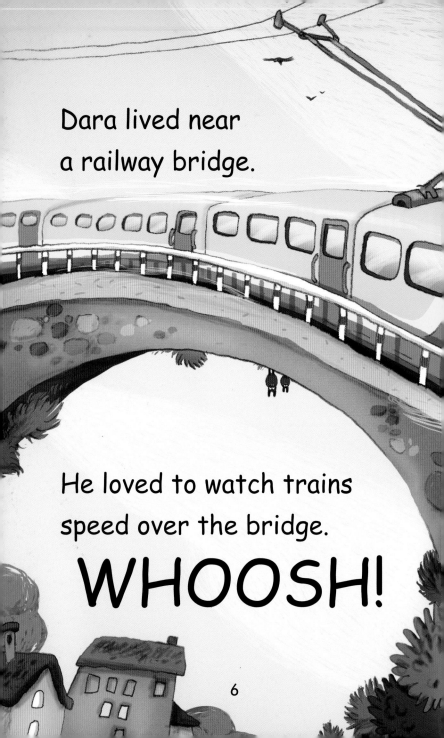

Dara lived near
a railway bridge.

He loved to watch trains
speed over the bridge.
WHOOSH!

He listened to the sound:
chicka-chicka, chicka-chicka.

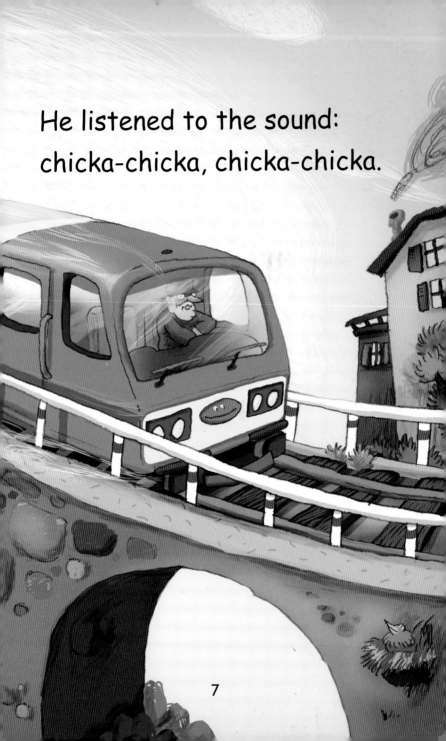

Dara had toy trains
and tracks.

He pushed his trains
over the bridge.

CHICKA-CHICKA

CHICKA-CHICKA

CHICKA-CHICKA

9

Uncle Joe told Dara
all about the trains
from long ago.

They were called
steam trains.

Steam trains made
a special noise:

chuff-chuff, chuff-chuff.

Steam came out the top.
And they had
a special whistle:

choo choo!

choo choo!

When Dara was five,
Uncle Joe gave him
a special birthday present.

It was a **steam train!**

'Wow!' said Dara.

He loved his steam train.
He played with it all day.

He even took it
to bed with him.

It was his favourite toy.

One day,
Dara's Mum and Dad
were going away.
They would be away
for two whole days.

Uncle Joe came
to look after Dara.

But Dara didn't want
Mum and Dad to go away.

Dara was very sad.
He played with his
steam train.

Uncle Joe made dinner,
but Dara wasn't hungry.
He had a pain in his tummy.

'I want Mum,' he said.
'Where is she?
Where's Dad?'

'Poor Dara,' said Uncle Joe.
'Don't worry. They'll be home
in two days.'

Next morning,
Dara was still very sad.

But Uncle Joe had
a special surprise for him.

'Come on, Dara,' he said.
'We're going
somewhere special!'
'Where?' said Dara.

'Wait and see,'
said Uncle Joe.

Uncle Joe took Dara
to the train station.
Dara stood on the platform.
He heard a train coming.

But it didn't sound like
the trains he heard
every day.
It had a special sound:

chuff-chuff, chuff-chuff.

Then, he saw it.
A big, red steam train!
He heard the whistle:

choo choo!

choo choo!

The steam train
puffed into the station.

'Hurray!' shouted Dara.

It stopped
right in front of Dara.
The driver got out.
It was Uncle Joe's
best friend, Ollie.

'Hello, Dara,' said Ollie.
'Are you ready to be
a train driver?'

'Me?' said Dara.
'A driver? Of a steam train!
Wow!'

Ollie lifted Dara
up on to the driver's seat.
He put his driver's cap
on Dara's head.

'Dara, the train driver!'
said Uncle Joe.

Dara forgot to be sad
about Mum and Dad.

Ollie walked
down the platform
and closed all the doors.

He pushed a big lever
and the steam train
began to move.

Slowly at first:
chuff ... chuff.

Then quicker and quicker:
chuff-chuff, chuff-chuff.

Soon the train
was speeding past the fields.

WHOOSH!

Dara waved at the cows
and sheep in the fields.

Then, up ahead,
he saw something
on the tracks.

It looked liked a sheep.

Oh no! They were going to
run over the sheep!

'Ollie,' he shouted.
'**Look out**!
There's a sheep
on the tracks!'

Ollie stared out.

'You're right, Dara!'
he said. 'We must
stop the train!'

'You pull that cord, Dara,'
said Ollie.
'I'll pull the lever.'

Uncle Joe helped Dara
pull hard on the cord.
The whistle went:
choo choo!

Ollie pulled the big lever.
The train began
to slow down.

Dara pulled the cord again:
choo choo!

And again:
choo choo!

The sheep heard the whistle
at last.

It looked up.
It saw the train coming!
It **ran off** the tracks.

'Wow!' said Ollie.
'That was close.
Well done, Dara,
for **spotting** that sheep!'

Ollie pushed the big lever.
The train began
to speed up again:

chuff-chuff, chuff-chuff.

Dara kept a good lookout
in case more sheep
went on the tracks.

WHOOSH!

The train sped along.

Dara couldn't stop smiling.
Uncle Joe couldn't
stop smiling.

'This is great!' said Dara.
'The best day ever!'

The next day,
Dara's Mum and Dad
came home.

Dara told them all about
the train and the sheep.

'Hey!' said Dad.
'You'd be a
great train driver,
Dara!'

Dara was very happy.
'I hope I can do it again!'

'Uncle Joe,' he said,
'can you look after me again
next week?'

'I'll see what I can do,'
said Uncle Joe.